·Favorite Fairy Tales·
Cinderella

Retold by Rochelle Larkin   **Illustrated by Alan Leiner**

The Playmore/Waldman® is a registered trademark of Playmore Inc. Publishers
and Waldman Publishing Corp., New York, New York

The Playmore/Waldman Bug Logo® is a registered trademark of Playmore Inc. Publishers
and Waldman Publishing Corp., New York, New York

Once upon a time in a faraway kingdom there lived a girl named Cinderella.

She was a good girl, but she had two sisters who were very mean to her.

The first sister was named Blasty. She yelled and screamed at Cinderella all day long and made her do all the cleaning and sweeping around the house.

The second sister was named Nasty. She did and said mean things to Cinderella all day long and made her do the cooking and laundry in the house.

   While Cinderella did all the work, Nasty and Blasty just
sat around, doing their hair and their nails and trying to make
themselves beautiful. But nothing helped!

Meanwhile, Cinderella, no matter how hard she worked, grew prettier and prettier.

One day, Cinderella was cleaning the house, sweeping in all the corners and under the furniture.

Suddenly, there was a knock at the door. Nasty and Blasty looked up in surprise. "Answer the door, Cinderella!" yelled Blasty.

Cinderella opened the door. A beautifully dressed young man stood in the doorway.

Cinderella tried to brush back her hair and smooth her dress, but Nasty and Blasty rushed right over, nearly knocking her down.

"What is it, what is it?" they asked, all excited.

The young man was a messenger from the palace. He unrolled the scroll from under his arm and began to read.

"By order of His Majesty, Prince Zohar, all citizens are invited to attend a grand ball at the palace this very night." Then he bowed, rolled up the scroll, and left.

Nasty and Blasty began to dance with joy. "The Prince! The Prince!" they shouted as they flung themselves around the room, singing and stamping their feet in tune to their own music.

"It's wonderful!" said Cinderella, her eyes shining.

The sisters stopped singing and dancing. They stared at her. "The ball isn't for you," cried Nasty. "Why, we would be ashamed to be seen with you!"

"Ashamed," yelled Blasty. "Prince Zohar is looking for a bride. He might choose one of us. You, a girl from the ashes and cinders, you would ruin our chances."

Cinderella went back to cleaning. She scrubbed very hard, polishing the big glass doorknob. But she couldn't stop her tears from falling. Soon there was a puddle of her tears on the floor.

She bent to wipe it up, but as she let go of the glass doorknob, it got big and light and bright. Cinderella stood back from the flashing light.

Suddenly, the bright light turned into a person. "Who are you?" Cinderella asked in a great fright.

The stout little woman straightened her tall pointy hat and smoothed out her dress. "Don't be afraid, Cinderella," she said. "I've come to help you. See this?"

She held up a long stick with a big star at the tip. "It's my magic wand."

Cinderella just stared in amazement.

"Now, you want to go to the ball," the little woman went on.

Cinderella nodded. She was too surprised to speak.

"There's a lot to do," the little woman said. "Let's go into the garden. I can get everything I need out there."

"Perfect! Perfect! Excellent!" said the little woman, pointing her magic wand in all directions. All at once an orange pumpkin turned into a golden coach and the dormice who tunneled their homes in the garden became a driver and attendants, all in glittering uniforms.

"I can't go to the ball like this," Cinderella said, looking down at her torn dress and bare feet.

"You're right," said the strange little woman. "I forgot the most important part. But not for long."

Suddenly Cinderella felt another flashing light shining all over her. She blinked. When she opened her eyes, she was wearing a long beautiful gown that sparkled all over. On her head was a jeweled crown and on her feet were perfect little glass slippers.

Cinderella tried to thank her, but the little woman waved her aside. "No time, no time, my dear," she said. "You have only till midnight."

"Midnight?" Cinderella echoed.

"Midnight!" the little woman said. "Then everything goes back to the way it was. Now into the coach with you, and don't forget."

When Cinderella arrived at the palace, every light was shining and beautiful music was playing. Many people were dancing in the crowded ballroom, but when Prince Zohar saw Cinderella, he came right to her.

They danced every dance. Cinderella had never been so happy. She floated on the Prince's arm as lightly as the music floated on the breeze.

Prince Zohar had never been so happy either. "What's your name?" he asked Cinderella as they danced. "I don't even know who you are!"

But just as she started to tell him, Cinderella heard the big palace clock strike twelve. It was midnight! She had been so happy she had forgotten.

She broke away from the Prince, allowing herself just one look at him before she ran up the great stairs and out of the palace.

Prince Zohar followed after her, but all he could find was a single glass slipper lying on the stairs. "I'll find her if we have to try this slipper on every girl in the kingdom!"

Cinderella was in her bed by the fire when Nasty and Blasty came home. She listened as they talked about the mysterious beauty who had danced with the prince and then disappeared.

But even more exciting was the search that would begin the very next morning. The prince would marry the girl whose foot fit into the glass slipper.

All the next day Nasty and Blasty kept Cinderella busy as they tried everything they could think of to make their feet smaller. But nothing helped.

They were still trying when the messenger came from the palace. Nasty and Blasty wiggled and wormed and squirmed but couldn't get more than a couple of toes in the slipper.

"Now let her try," said the messenger as he saw Cinderella sitting in the shadows.

"Not her! She's nobody!" yelled Blasty and Nasty.

But Cinderella came forward smiling, and of course, the slipper was a perfect fit.

Prince Zohar himself came back to claim Cinderella for his bride. And they lived happily ever after.